Praise for
Sally Warner's *Lily* books.

"The most charming, pain-in-the-neck kid since Beverly Cleary's Ramona." —*Buffalo News*

"Warner keeps the tone light and the focus tight....The childlike first-person narration is written with considerable humor and grace." —*Kirkus Reviews*

"Lily's humorous, first-person narrative will have great appeal for young children....A charming chapter book that should be a popular choice for reading aloud." —*Booklist*

"Lily is as emotionally sensitive as Ramona and a little less precocious than Junie B. Jones, but with similar misunderstandings and conflicts about life. Warner knows what's important to young children and has a good ear for dialogue. Readers will nod in recognition of Lily's problems."
　　　　　　　　　　　　　—*School Library Journal*

Also by Sally Warner:

Dog Years

Some Friend

Ellie & the Bunheads

Sort of Forever

Other books about Lily:

Sweet & Sour Lily

Private Lily

Accidental Lily

LEFTOVER LILY

Sally Warner

illustrated by
Jacqueline Rogers

A Knopf Paperback
Alfred A. Knopf
New York

For Nan Cannon

A KNOPF PAPERBACK PUBLISHED BY ALFRED A. KNOPF

www.randomhouse.com/kids

Library of Congress Cataloging-in-Publication Data
Warner, Sally.
Leftover Lily / by Sally Warner ; illustrated by Jacqueline Rogers.
p.   cm.
Summary: When first-grader Lily gets into a fight with her two best
friends, the experience teaches her a lot about friendship.
[1. Friendship—Fiction. 2. Best friends—Fiction. 3. Schools—Fiction.]
I. Rogers, Jacqueline, ill. II. Title.
PZ7.W24644Le   1999
[Fic]—dc21   98-11669

ISBN   0-679-89139-0 (trade)
0-679-99139-5 (lib. bdg.)
0-375-80347-5 (pbk.)

First Knopf Paperback edition: April 2000
Printed in the United States of America
10 9 8 7 6 5 4 3 2

CONTENTS

CHAPTER ONE
What Happened?

"Go away for a second, Lily. There's something I have to ask LaVon," Daisy says. We are playing outside after lunch, the same as usual.

My heart goes *floop*. Up until now, the three of us have shared everything. "Go ahead and ask her—I don't care," I say, shrugging.

"No, it's private," Daisy says, and she smiles and shakes her head. Her shiny yellow hair swings back and forth, like in a shampoo commercial.

LaVon's dark eyes go from me to Daisy. "You can ask me later on," she finally says to Daisy. "Let's all go play now. The bell is going to ring pretty soon."

Daisy scowls and gives me a dirty look.

Me! And I have just shared my peanut butter celery with her!

I share because her mother packs such terrible lunches that Daisy would starve if LaVon and I weren't so nice!

But we *are* nice, because we're friends with stupid Daisy!

"I have to talk to LaVon *now*," Daisy says to me. "Go over there, by the fence. Just for a minute." She is starting to get mad.

I feel my face get hot. "You're not the boss of me," I say to Daisy. "You can't tell me where to stand and what to do."

Now Daisy is the one to shrug. "Well, I'm doing it, aren't I?" she asks me.

That *sounds* like a question, but it is the kind of question that really isn't a question. So you don't have to answer it.

"Tell me later," LaVon says to Daisy, almost begging her. "Come on, let's play."

"Nuh-uh—it's important for me to tell you now," Daisy says.

I want to say, *Hey, we were best friends just a minute ago! What happened?* But instead I say, "I'm not moving. And you're just being dumb. Also, very mean."

A smile flies across Daisy's face so fast that I almost don't see it. I think she *likes* fighting! She reaches out and tugs at LaVon's hot-pink slicker. "Come on, LaVon, let's go somewhere we can get some privacy," she says.

LaVon looks confused. "But-but-but-" she sputters. She starts to be pulled away from me, though, *hop-hop-hop*.

Just the way Daisy wants.

So I grab hold of LaVon's other arm and start pulling her back.

"Let go of her!" Daisy orders me.

"*You* let go!" I order back. Hah! She's not the only one who can be bossy!

"No, you!" Daisy shouts. She gives LaVon's arm a great big yank, and then—I guess Daisy's hand slips on the raincoat or something, because all of a sudden it lets go of the sleeve and Daisy goes sprawling onto the playground.

"Ow!" Daisy yells.

But she isn't really hurt. You can tell.

"Oh—are you okay?" LaVon asks Daisy, forgetting all about me. I look up and see the playground teacher walking toward us fast, the way grownups do when they are in a big hurry but they don't want to look silly by running.

Daisy sees the teacher, too. *"Wahhh!"* She starts to cry, squeezing out a few tears.

I back away a step or two.

"What's going on here?" the play-ground teacher says, puffing a little. "Are you okay?" she asks Daisy. "Did somebody push you?" The woman looks at me and LaVon like we are muggers or something.

"She just fell, that's all," LaVon says, helping Daisy up.

The woman sniffs. "Well," she says, "you didn't bang your head, did you?"

"I—I don't *think* so," Daisy says, trying to sound as if she might have. Because when your head gets banged on the play-ground, teachers pay attention.

And Daisy *loves* attention.

She rubs at the back of her head like maybe it is feeling just a little bit sore.

"I'd better take you to see the nurse," the playground teacher says. She is frowning, as

6

though Daisy has fallen down just to ruin her lunch hour.

"No, I'll be okay," Daisy says. She is trying to sound brave now.

Zzzz! The bell rings.

"You two go on back to class," the woman says to me and LaVon.

But we stand there and watch her lead Daisy away. Daisy's limp keeps changing from one side to the other. I guess she is trying to figure out what she is going to tell the school nurse.

"Good, she's gone," I say, sneaking a look at LaVon.

"Huh!" LaVon says, scowling at me. She whirls around and starts walking to class alone.

And all of a sudden I am alone, too.

CHAPTER TWO
Leftover Lily

It is the morning after the playground fight, and my big brother Casey is driving me nuts! "I did *not* get up on the wrong side of the bed," I tell him. "There is only one side I can get up on, because the other side is my special folding frog screen. *Duh.*"

Case laughs the kind of laugh that says, *Boy, are you dumb!* "Frogs don't fold," he says, trying to make a joke. "And saying someone got up on the wrong side of the bed is just an expression," he informs me. "It means—"

"I know it's an expression," I fib, interrupting him. "You just *expressed* it, didn't you?" I jump up from the kitchen table, and I accidentally knock my chair over. *Clunk!*

The rain is pounding down outside. Oh, great! This is the first February that we have ever lived in Philadelphia, and so far I hate it. Valentine's Day is going to be terrible this year. Usually it's my favorite.

It smells like burned toast in the kitchen. "Casey, Lily," Mommy says, looking up from her newspaper. She sighs, puts the paper down, and then holds her arms out to me. I get pulled into her hug as if she is some kind of magical magnet, a *mommy*-magnet. She pats me on the back, and I sneak a look at Case.

He is pretending not to notice that I am the one getting all the cuddles around here.

Sometimes he acts like he is almost grown-up, but I know that he still keeps track of who is getting the hugs and stuff. Even though he is twelve years old.

I sniffle. "Casey's teasing me," I say, sounding tiny and sad.

Case gets all huffy. "Mom—"

"Oh, Lily," Mommy says, cutting off his words, "toughen up, sweetie."

"I'm only six!" I tell her. I'm pretty sure that she remembers that, so how can she expect me to be tough?

Mommy ruffles my mouse-brown hair and squeezes me tight. "Quit it," I say, pulling away—but only a little.

"Casey only means that you've been acting grouchy all morning," Mommy says.

"I have not," I say, snuggling closer into Mommy's lap. I am trying to act the opposite of grouchy now, just so I can show how wrong Casey is.

"You have *too* been acting grouchy!" Case says, almost pouncing on my words. "What about screaming at me when I knocked on the bathroom door?"

"You were pounding on it, and *you* were bothering *me,*" I tell him. I was busy in there counting my freckles in the mirror, but I keep that part private.

"Well, you were hogging," he says.

Mommy stands up and pours me off her lap, as if she is a bulldozer. She pushes her hands back through her hair. *Uh-oh.*

But Casey doesn't see her getting mad. He is still saying his list of how crabby I am. "Well, what about yelling at me when I poured myself a glass of milk?" he asks.

"You were using it all up! I need milk for my cereal," I say back, fast. *"Duh!"* It is a well-known fact that I eat cereal for breakfast every day.

"You two quit squabbling this *instant*," Mommy tells us. She carries her half-empty mug of tea to the sink and stands with her back to us, looking down at the dirty plates and bowls. She is not using good posture. I think she is sad.

"*Now* look what you did," Case mutters to me.

"I did not!" I mutter back, and I am so angry that I throw my cereal spoon across the table. Nobody can make me as mad as my brother can.

"Lily!" my mommy shouts while the spoon is still in the air.

"Ow!" Casey yells, even though it misses him by a mile. That faker.

"Quit ganging up on me!" I yell at both

of them. I run into the bathroom, which is the only *really* private place in our whole apartment.

I slam the door shut behind me. Mommy and Casey are being so unfair! I am *not* acting grouchy this morning. I'm acting like my normal everyday self.

But in the bathroom, my eyes get hot— the way they do right before I start to cry. I can hardly stand to even *think* about going to school after what happened yesterday.

Daisy acts like she's so great.

So instead of thinking about school, I climb up on the yellow plastic footstool in front of the sink and stare into the mirror for the second time this morning. I'll count the rest of my freckles.

Twenty-three, twenty-four—no, wait, I already counted that one ...

The rain is splashing down over Mommy's umbrella, like someone is squirting a hose on us. Mommy and I try to stay inside our little dry space under the umbrella as we move along, but it is not easy. The wind tugs the umbrella every which way and sometimes blows the rain right into our faces or against our shivery backs.

My mommy walks me to school every day. I am in the first grade at Betsy Ross Primary School. I am very popular there and have a lot of friends.

Well, okay, that is not exactly the truth— but at least nobody hated me up until now! Even my teacher, Ms. Marshall, likes me.

Ms. Marshall is pretty, Daisy and LaVon and I decided last fall, but she also gets nervous sometimes for no reason. Just from being around us kids, I guess.

I am a medium-smart kid in class. Not as smart as Marcus, who sits next to me, but almost as smart as Hilary, a shy girl who sits near the window. Hilary can count to one hundred by twos. I heard her do it once.

I have the medium amount of friends, which is two good ones. Or I did have two friends—until yesterday after lunch.

But Daisy Greenough and LaVon Hamilton have been *best* friends with each other for a long time, that's the problem! In fact, they were friends when I still lived in New Jersey. No fair.

"Lily, don't splash," Mommy says to me. One of my yellow rain boots has just landed in a puddle. There are lots of holes in the sidewalk around here.

"I didn't splash," I say to her. "And anyway, it's not *my* fault it's raining."

Mommy moves the umbrella a little to cover me better. "Boy," she says, "you *did* get up on the wrong side of the bed."

"Stop saying that!" I yell.

"Well, then, what is your problem?" Mommy asks me.

When people ask, *What is your problem?* they are really saying, *Quit acting like that!* They don't really want to know if you are sad or anything.

It is not what I call a real question. So why should I give it a real answer?

"*Nothing* is my problem," I tell her. "Everything is perfectly perfect, just like on a TV show."

"Huh," Mommy says. "If it's the six o'clock news, maybe."

Good—she doesn't believe me. But who cares? "We don't have to walk so fast," I say, because I don't *ever* want to get to school.

"Yes we do, or you'll be late for school and I'll be late for work," she says.

"Well, I don't care if I'm late. And I'm tired of your stupid work! You never have enough time for me anymore. And I hate it how you're always in a hurry," I tell her. She feels bad whenever I say these three things.

"Oh, Lily, I'm sorry," Mommy tells me, right on schedule. Her big shoulder bag slips, and she stops to sling the strap over her head and across her chest. Inside the bag is her lunch and all her important papers for work, which is in a bookstore.

I stop, too, and hunch my own backpack up higher.

"Sweetheart," Mommy says, starting to walk again, "is there something about school that is making you sad?"

I shake my head *no,* and the hood of my smelly yellow raincoat falls back.

"Well, then," Mommy says, trying again, "are you feeling all right? Do you think you might have a fever?"

"No!" I say. There is no point in lying about a fever. They will only take your temperature, and then what?

We walk along *splish-splosh* for a while, not saying anything more. I am going as slow as I dare.

"Well," Mommy says again as we get close to Betsy Ross, "when you're ready, I hope you'll talk to me about whatever is bothering you."

Parents like to say that, I think,

because then they feel as though they have helped you—even if they haven't. "Yeah, okay, sure," I say. But I'm not really going to tell her what happened.

And I am not even thinking about my words. Instead, I am busy looking through the raindrops for Daisy and LaVon. They are probably together, and they are probably having a wonderful time.

Without me.

Because one thing I learned yesterday is that it is easy for two kids to be best friends, but it is harder for three kids to do it. And three minus two equals one, which is what will be left over.

That's me, leftover Lily.

CHAPTER THREE
Something a Little Different

"Move it, stupid-face," Stevie Braddock says to me in the cloakroom, like always.

"You're the stupid-face," I say back at him, like always.

Stevie *sounds* mean, but he's okay, really. He is the biggest boy in our class, and he is best friends with Marcus— who is also okay, even though he teases me.

Ollie Howard is the one you have to watch out for. Him and Daisy.

Daisy and LaVon aren't even here yet, so I don't have to put a careful expression on my face. "Stupid-face," I say again to Stevie. He looks at me, surprised. Usually we only say it one time each.

"Oh, yeah?" he says. He looks like he doesn't know what to do next.

"Yeah," I say. I take off my rain boots, pull my red sneakers out of my backpack, and try to lean against the wall to put them on. I lean right against a drippy raincoat, and my behind gets all wet.

Oh, perfect! Now I will have to listen to kids make lame jokes all morning about me wetting my pants. Which never really happens anymore. Maybe I got up on the wrong side of the *day*.

The real trouble around here is Daisy— how bossy she is. Or how bossy her mom is. Mrs. Greenough is our room mother this year, and she thinks she is the queen of the world. She tells all the other parents that they have to send healthy snacks for the class to share when it is somebody's birthday, so we almost choke on these weird dry cupcakes with no frosting on them when we are trying to sing "Happy Birthday to You." Stuff like that.

And some of her mom's bossiness has rubbed off on Daisy. See, I think it is like what would happen if your mother was covered with blue poster paint. No matter how careful you tried to be, you would get blue on you! That is my explanation for it.

Usually I don't mind that Daisy is a little bossy because usually it is not me who she bosses around. But she sure tried to do it yesterday!

"What happened? Did you wet your pants?" Marcus asks, grinning.

"Yeah, and if you're not careful, I'm going to wet *yours*," I tell him. I flop into my seat. That ought to shut him up.

But oh, no. "Hey," he says, "I heard you pushed Daisy down in the playground. Way to go! Serves her right."

Daisy is walking to her seat now, as though Marcus has made her appear just by saying her name. I think she heard him.

She doesn't even look at me.

"I did not push Daisy down," I say in a very loud voice. "She fell, that's all."

"Oh, sure," Marcus says, also real loud.

LaVon walks by, just as the bell rings. She is wearing a yellow and white striped dress today, and there are tiny matching yellow barrettes at the ends of her three braids. LaVon has the cutest clothes.

She doesn't look at me, either.

Ms. Marshall claps her hands three times. "Okay, boys and girls, settle down," she says. "Come get your arithmetic workbook when I call your name." And she starts taking roll in alphabetical order.

"Lily Hill!" Ms. Marshall says, and I march up to the front of the room. I wish I had worn my new red sweater today instead of this old shirt that has the baggy turtleneck.

Daisy whispers something to LaVon and they nod, their faces serious.

"Now, class," Ms. Marshall says when we are all seated again, "we're going to try something a little different this morning."

A wiggle of excitement passes through the room, but I am suspicious about this news. After all, I am holding my arithmetic workbook, aren't I? Whatever we do, it will probably have something to do with counting fruit. Or pennies.

We never count both at the same time.

No one ever asks, *What do you get when you add three oranges and two pennies?*

Now, *that* would be a little different.

Even when we only count fruit, though, I hate it how they always make you give the simplest answer. Whenever the picture-question is asking what you get when you add two apples, say, and three apples, they want you to say five apples. But my answer is—*It all depends!*

It all depends if those things are really supposed to be apples! They always draw them funny, all crooked in the middle and with leaves attached. I have never seen leaves on apples in the store we go to.

So what *are* those things?

"Lily, are you paying any attention to me at *all?*" Ms. Marshall says, standing behind me. I jump a little—which is not easy to do when you are sitting down.

"Lily is busy flexing her muscles," Marcus tells the world. "I guess she's getting ready to beat somebody up at recess."

All the kids have heard about Daisy falling down yesterday in the playground, and so everybody laughs. Everybody except Ms. Marshall, that is. "Shut up," I whisper to Marcus.

"That's enough, Mr. Webster," Ms. Marshall says. She has started calling Marcus *Mr. Webster* whenever he goofs off. Which is a lot of the time, because he always finishes his work too early and then looks around for some trouble to get into.

"Yeah, *Mr. Webster,*" I whisper. Marcus starts to swing his pointy elbow in my direction, but Ms. Marshall puts her hand on his shoulder and he stops, like she has frozen him with an ice ray. I know all about ice

rays because I read Casey's comic books.

"As I was saying," Ms. Marshall says, keeping one hand on Marcus, "we're going to try something new. I want you to work in pairs today."

At first I think she means pears, like the kind you eat, and I am thinking, *So what? It's still fruit!* But when she starts calling our names out two at a time, I get it.

"Stevie Braddock and LaVon Hamilton," she calls out.

Huh, I think, as LaVon and Stevie stand up and get ready to walk over to the window, to the place where Ms. Marshall is pointing for them to go.

"Bring your workbooks and pencils," she reminds them. "Daisy Greenough and Ollie Howard," Ms. Marshall says next.

Hah!

"Hilary Mitchell and Lily Hill."

Hilary! I barely even *know* her. But I grab my workbook and my sharpest pencil, and I trot over to stand next to shy and quiet Hilary, with her long skinny braids and her scared round eyes.

Daisy shrinks away from me when I walk past, like I am going to bop her one.

And Hilary is looking very nervous as I stand next to her. "Hello," I say, to show her how nice I really am. I smile, showing most of my teeth.

She takes a step back. "Hi," she whispers. This is practically the most I have heard Hilary say all year. She used to play with Shawna Collins, who sat behind her, but then Shawna moved to Arizona after Christmas vacation.

Hilary should be *glad* that I'm her

partner for fruit math! I smile at her again, and she fiddles with the end of a braid. "Don't keep backing up or you'll crash through the window," I say to her, which is very good advice.

"Now, after you sit down with your partner," Ms. Marshall says, "I want you each to complete page forty-six in the workbook. And then you will trade workbooks and correct each other's answers!" She says this like it is a happy surprise.

Muh-muh-muh, everyone grumbles as we sit down in strange seats. I *guess* this is new and different, but in my opinion we are only doing it so that Ms. Marshall won't have to correct our work. A couple of kids look at me. I guess they want to see if I have knocked Hilary over yet.

I sigh, and I try to answer all the questions

the way the workbook people want me to—
without ever thinking, *It all depends!*

Even though someone has drawn the
oranges with speckly dots all over them
for some reason. And even though they
want you to count *bunches* of grapes
instead of every single grape. And even
though the apples are drawn funny again,
with leaves on them.

Marcus finishes first, as usual, and he
gets busy bothering his partner, who is a
girl named Lupe. She is getting mad at him,
you can tell.

I finish second. I wait politely for Hilary
to finish, too. She is slower than usual
today, for some reason. When she stops
writing, we trade workbooks. She bends
her head low over my page forty-six and
starts correcting.

I sneak a look and notice that she is drawing a big, curly *C* next to every one of my correct answers. That looks cool, almost like cursive writing! And so I make an even curlier *C* next to one of her correct answers.

Hilary sees what I am doing and sneaks me a very fast smile.

I smile back, also very fast.

Hilary spies another correct answer on my worksheet, and she makes an extra-fancy *C* now—just like mine, but with a lit-tle flower in the middle!

I make a flower inside of a *C* on her page, too.

We smile at each other again, slower this time. *Hey,* I am thinking, *maybe Hilary can be a whole new friend for me!*

I look over at mean LaVon, who is

scowling suspiciously while she watches Stevie mark up her worksheet. She is very fussy about keeping her pages neat.

I look over at bossy Daisy, who is trying to have a quiet argument with Ollie about one of her answers. "Don't you dare mark that answer wrong!" she is scolding him.

He shrugs, grins at her, and makes a sloppy line of big old *X*s that I can see from three desks away. "Wrong, wrong, wrong!" he sings out.

"They are *not* wrong!" Daisy tries to yell under her breath.

Then I look at Hilary, who is peacefully decorating another *C. She's perfect,* I decide. Why was I ever friends with Daisy and LaVon in the first place? With Hilary, *I'm* the one who will get to be the boss.

I can hardly wait!

CHAPTER FOUR
Chain Link

"Do you want to eat lunch tog[...] Hilary in the cloakroom. I say it as though I don't care what the answer is.

Hilary's eyes jump to where Daisy and LaVon are standing. They are whispering together, and I see LaVon give Daisy a little nudge with her elbow. Daisy hesitates, but then takes a step in my direction.

Oh, no—she's going to yell at me in front of everyone! And our whole class is already on her side of the fight, which didn't even start out to be a fight, if you ask me.

But nobody is asking me anything.

Stevie did *call* me something a few minutes ago, though. *Slugger.*

"Come on," I say to Hilary, and I grab her

35

and pull her out of the cloakroom, fast. She didn't say that she wanted to eat with me, but I decided for her.

* * *

It has stopped raining, so I tell her that we should eat near the trash cans. Nobody usually eats there, but it has gotten pretty cold out, so the cans don't stink today—very much, anyway.

"Why here?" Hilary asks, looking around. Her regular talking voice sounds a little croaky. She fiddles with one of her braids again.

"There's nothing wrong with *here*," I inform her. "This is where I eat lunch all the time."

Hilary blinks at this lie—which she must know is a lie—but all she says is, "Well, but where are we supposed to sit?"

"We *stand*," I say, sounding very sure of myself. I figure that Hilary will probably let me boss her around if it seems like I know what I'm doing. "Here, lean against the fence," I tell her.

Hilary leans carefully against the chain-link fence—which is still very cold and drippy from this morning.

"What did you bring for lunch today?" I say, trying to sound like we are having a normal conversation. I look at Hilary's brown paper bag. It seems very large for such a skinny kid.

Hilary blushes. "You know, just regular stuff," she says softly.

"Like what?" I ask. "Show me." It is as if I am trying out my bossiness to see how it fits!

Being bossy still feels a little weird, but maybe I will get used to it.

Still blushing, Hilary pulls out a small square plastic bag. "There's this," she says.

"What kind is it?" I ask, staring at the yummy-looking sandwich inside.

"Roast chicken," she says, sounding guilty. And then, as if she has decided to get it all over with fast, she adds, "I also have a thingy full of pasta salad and some homemade chocolate cake."

"Chocolate cake?" I ask. I think about my own Fig Newtons that looked so great when Mommy packed them this morning.

Hilary nods, miserable.

"Wow," I say. "Your mom is a good cook. She must not have a job," I add. Because I bet my mommy would make chocolate cake if she didn't have a job.

"Yes, she does *too* have a job," Hilary

says. "But anyway, my daddy's the one who makes my lunches."

I stare at her, forgetting my own lunch for a second. *My* daddy only cooked frozen waffles—when he lived with us. But they were good. They were very, very good.

"My daddy's a chef," Hilary is saying.

"Huh? What's a chef?" I ask her. "Is that like a chief or something?"

Hilary smiles, which makes her whole face look different. "Kind of," she says. "It's like he's the chief cook. You know, in a restaurant."

"A *fancy* one?" I ask her. Case is always saying that he wants to take Mommy out for dinner to a fancy restaurant, but he hasn't done it yet.

"Yeah, I guess it's pretty fancy," Hilary

says. She takes out part of her sandwich. "Want to share?" she asks me.

I crinkle my paper bag, as if I am reading its mind with my fingertips. "I only have plain old tuna fish on plain white bread," I finally admit. "And a regular mom made it, not a chef."

"That's okay," Hilary says, giggling. "I like plain tuna fish. And I get tired of chef food sometimes."

I munch on my half of the chicken sandwich while I think about this. Out of the corner of my eye I see Daisy and LaVon link their arms together and skip across the playground. Hilary sees them, too, and she clears her throat. "Can I ask you a question?" she says, sounding nervous.

Which makes me remember that she has *not* sounded nervous ever since we started leaning on the fence. In fact, she has sounded almost happy!

And that is okay, as long as she knows who is the boss around here.

"Go ahead and ask," I say, trying to sound like I am still in charge. I frown a little.

Hilary leans back against the fence when she sees me frown, but she says really fast, "I-just-wanted-to-know-if-you-really-punched-Daisy-in-the-face-like-everyone-says, that's all. But maybe she deserved it!"

I feel my mouth hang open, like I am a surprised person in a Saturday morning cartoon show. Then I clack it shut. "I never punched her," I say.

"Well, *hit* her, then," Hilary says.

"I never hit her, either," I say. "We were both pulling on LaVon, and Daisy fell, that's all."

"Oh," Hilary says, and she looks a little—*disappointed?* But why would she be sorry that I didn't really haul off and sock Daisy?

Daisy and LaVon skip by again, closer this time. It is almost like they want me to see them having fun. "Are you finished eating yet?" I ask Hilary.

"Mmph," she says, and slurps a curly noodle into her mouth.

"Well, hurry up," I boss her, "because I want to skip."

Hilary swallows hard, like she is eating lumpy popcorn balls at Halloween and not cold slithery noodles when it is almost Valentine's Day.

Valentine's Day—which is next Monday.

And my two best friends hate me!

I give Hilary another toothy smile. I will just have to work hard at being friends with her, I guess, so I will not be all alone on Valentine's Day. "I'm not a very good skipper," Hilary tells me.

"I'll teach you," I say in a special way that lets her know she had better say, *Thanks,* if she knows what's good for her!

"Thanks," Hilary says, sighing a little. She dumps the rest of her pasta salad in the trash, which is easy to do because we are standing right next to the cans. "Okay, let's skip," she says gloomily.

And so we link our arms, too, and off we go, stumble-skipping across the playground—gritting our teeth and trying to act like we are friends.

CHAPTER FIVE
Kind of a Pain

"Knock, knock!" I say that night, pretending to rap on Case's fake bedroom door. Case's room is almost like a cave at the end of our living room. Inside the cave are a bed and a table that holds his books and a clock radio. That's all there is space for in there. But it is private, because there is a red and white striped curtain that divides the bed from the rest of the room.

"Who's there?" Case calls out.

"It's Arnold Schwarzenegger," I tell him.

Case *knows* who is knocking, but he always asks, for some reason.

"Sorry, Arnold, I'm busy!" Case says.

I'm pretty sure that he is drawing in there. Case is a really good cartooner.

"Okay, okay. It's me, Lily," I say. "Come on, Case, let me in—it's important!"

Casey sweeps the curtain open, like he is a wizard granting a wish. "You may approach the throne," he tells me. I climb up on the end of his bed, and he leans over and pulls the curtain shut behind me. It smells good inside, like the last cozy reminder of the hamburgers and Tater Tots we had for dinner. And ketchup.

We were supposed to eat peas, too, but no way. I hid mine.

"What are you drawing?" I ask him, trying to peek.

"Nothing," he says, slamming his notebook shut. "What's so important, anyway?"

"Oh, just something at school," I mumble, smoothing down a wrinkle in his blue bedspread.

"What?" he asks, cupping his hand behind his ear like a cartoon old guy. "Speak up, I can't hear you!"

"I *said,* it was just something at school!" I yell.

Mommy is in the living room talking on the phone. She calls, "Are you two all right?" which really means *Stop fighting!*

"We're fine," Casey and I sing out.

We look at each other, and Case puts an inky finger to his lips. "Shhh," he warns me.

"You *shhh,*" I warn him back. "You're the one," I say.

Case sighs and taps his fingers on his notebook. Uh-oh, I can tell that he wishes he could start drawing again. I had better start talking—fast. "I had a fight with Daisy yesterday," I say.

"What kind of a fight?" he asks. The

corner of his mouth looks like it is trying not to smile.

He'd better *not* smile! This is serious. "What do you mean, what kind of fight?" I ask him.

"Well, did Daisy look at you funny and hurt your feelings? Did she steal your cookies? What *kind* of a fight?" he repeats.

"She bossed me around," I tell him.

"Daisy bosses everyone around," Casey points out. See, he's met Daisy before. He knows what she's like.

"Yeah, but usually not me," I say. "And Daisy wanted to whisper a secret to LaVon, which wasn't very nice! And so we started tugging on LaVon. And so Daisy slipped, that's all. And so she fell down on her rear end. And so everyone thinks that I pushed her!"

"Wait a minute—hold on," Case says, raising his hand. He scrunches up his face, as though he is trying to picture the fight. "You and Daisy were *pulling on LaVon?*" He says it real slow.

I nod.

"Like she was a *wishbone?*" Case asks. Now his mouth is *really* trying not to smile.

"Well, we didn't want to pull her apart," I say, kind of grouchy. "I don't exactly remember why we started pulling, in fact. But nobody got hurt."

"Okay, so then what happened? Did you get busted?" Case asks me. He isn't even thinking of drawing now.

"Nuh-uh," I say, shaking my head. "It ended up that the playground teacher didn't blame me, but when I came to school today everyone was acting like I was this tough guy and everything."

"Huh," Case says, looking at me as if I am telling a great big lie.

I am kind of weensy, I have to admit! I am not the first person you would think of when you hear the words *tough guy*.

"Anyway, Daisy and LaVon aren't even talking to me now," I say. I can feel my chin start to wobble, the way it does right before I cry. "The only girl who will play with me is Hilary Mitchell. With the *braids*." I don't mention to Case about bossing Hilary around all afternoon.

"Well, did you tell Daisy that you were sorry?" Case asks me.

"I'm not sorry!" I tell him. "Why should I be sorry? I didn't do anything! Daisy's the one who was being mean—to me!"

"Yeah, but you're not the one who fell down," Case says.

"That was her own fault!" I say, trying not to yell.

But Mommy's ears can hear even whisper fighting. "Are you two doing okay in there?" she calls out, sounding a little bit mad this time.

"We're fine," Case and I say together, and then we *shhh* each other some more.

We sit there for a minute, quiet. Then Case says, "So what do you want from me?"

"I want you to tell me how to get everyone in class to stop blaming me for the whole thing!" I tell him.

"They're *all* mad at you?" Case asks.

I think about this. "Well, no," I finally admit, "it's more like they think Daisy and I are having this huge fight and can't stand each other now. So they're excited. You know, they're saying, *Way to go!* to me and stuff like that."

"Huh," Case says. "Everyone must really hate Daisy a lot. She *is* kind of a pain."

"She is not!" I say, pounding on his bed-spread so hard that his notebook slides off his lap. "She's . . . Daisy is just a little bit bossy sometimes," I tell him. "But she's my friend. Or she *was* my friend."

Case runs his hands back through his shaggy brown hair, which—*uh-oh*— means that he is getting bored with me. "Well, is Daisy still mad?" he asks, picking up his notebook again.

"I-I-I-" I have trouble answering this question. Because is Daisy still mad? "I don't know," I finally say to Casey.

"If she's not mad, then you don't really

have a problem. Can't you find out?" he says to me. "What about asking LaVon Hamilton?" Case has met LaVon before, too.

"I guess I could call her up," I say slowly, "but what if LaVon yells at me on the phone and I find out that Daisy still hates me? I'll feel so bad!"

Casey shrugs. "Well, you feel bad *now*," he points out.

"Yeah," I admit. "This whole thing makes me hurt—right here," I say, grabbing at my stomach.

"So call LaVon," Case says. "Before it's *too late*," he adds, which sounds very scary. He picks up his felt-tip pen as if it is a magic wand and he is about to make me disappear.

The telephone receiver is still hot from when Mommy was using it. She tells me

LaVon's telephone number from the class list. I punch the right buttons. A man answers the phone.

"Hi," I say. "Mr. Hamilton? Can I please speak with LaVon? *May* I speak with LaVon," I correct myself after catching the look that Mommy gives me. "This is Lily Hill," I add politely.

"Oh, hello, Lily," LaVon's daddy says. "I'm sorry, but I think that LaVon is already in bed. Her mama is reading her a story right now. But I'll tell her you called, honey."

It's very clear that he is about to hang up. "No, wait, please," I say to him, "can't I talk to her just for a minute? I have to ask her something. Something *important.*"

"Is it about school?"

"Y-e-s-s-s," I say slowly. Well, it is, kind of.

"I'll go get her, then," LaVon's daddy

says, and he puts the telephone down. I can hear his footsteps leave the room.

And then I hear LaVon. "Lily?" she says, sounding a little confused. "Is that you?"

"Oh, *hi,* LaVon," I say, as if she was the one who called me. "How are you?"

"Fine, thanks," she says, and then she is quiet.

I try to think of what to say next. "Are you still sore from when me and Daisy pulled on you like a ... like a wishbone?" I ask, stealing Casey's word.

Because it's a funny word!

Sure enough, LaVon gives a little laugh. "No," she says, "but I *wish* you guys would never do that again."

"We won't," I say to her. "I mean *I* won't, anyway. I can't promise you about Daisy."

"Oh," LaVon says.

"Is she still mad at me?" I ask—before I forget how brave I'm trying to be.

"Yeah, kind of," LaVon says. "You ruined her surprise."

"What surprise?"

I can almost see LaVon shrug before she answers. "Oh, she was going to have us over for a little party where we could make Valentine's Day cards," she says. "You know, to give out in class—with glitter and everything. But now the whole thing is ruined, just because of you. It won't be a party if it's just two people, only Daisy and me." LaVon sounds sad. She *loves* parties. "Daisy even got these special stickers for us to use on the valentines," she adds.

Stickers! *I* love stickers. "But—but how come Daisy wanted me to go away?

Right before we started pulling on you?"
I ask.

"Well, she wanted to find out if you still had to go to the baby-sitter on Saturdays while your mom works," LaVon tells me. "She was trying to figure out what day to have the party, on Saturday or on Sunday."

"But why didn't she just *ask* me?" I wail.

"How should I know?" LaVon wails right back at me. "First she told you to go away, and next thing I know, you guys were having this big old fight!"

"But I didn't push her down," I remind LaVon.

"I know that," LaVon says.

"But everyone in our whole class thinks I did," I say.

"I know."

"Well, can't you tell them that I didn't push her?" I ask her.

LaVon sighs. "Okay, I'll try," she says, "but I don't think they care what *really* happened."

She's right about that. Stevie and Marcus love it when they even *think* that there's a fight going on in our class. It doesn't matter if the rumor is true or not.

Now I'm the one to sigh. "And tell Daisy I'm sorry about wrecking her surprise," I say to LaVon.

"*You* tell her," LaVon says. "If you're not too busy playing with your new friend *Hilary,* that is." LaVon actually sounds a little bit—jealous!

"Hilary's pretty nice," I say, rubbing it in.

"Huh," LaVon says. "Whenever I tried to play with her before Christmas, she was always busy with *Shawna.*

"And anyway," LaVon adds, "it doesn't even matter—because I don't even know if Daisy is still going to invite me over to make cards. She might not be in the mood anymore."

Daisy always has to be in the mood for stuff.

So now I know another reason why LaVon is sounding sad. She *loves* making art, especially when you get to use glitter! "I'm sorry I accidentally wrecked the party," I tell her.

"Try telling that to Daisy," she says, which is the second time she had said that I should tell Daisy something.

"Okay," I agree. "I'll try."

But I know it's not going to be easy— because the truth is, Daisy is not the type of person you can tell stuff to!

CHAPTER SIX

A Cloudy Day

It is almost time for nutrition break, and I am very hungry. I have planned what I am going to eat, which is triangles of pita bread and long thready strips of string cheese. Yum.

Hilary's chef-daddy probably made her something wonderful to eat. Maybe I can boss her into sharing!

LaVon probably has a sack of peanut butter and jelly crackers, because that is her favorite morning snack. She is a good sharer, with no bossing or begging.

And Daisy—well, Daisy shares, too, even though we don't really ask her to. Daisy's not allergic to nuts or anything, the way Stevie Braddock is, but Mrs. Greenough is still bossy about her food the same way she is bossy about everything.

Here are some of the weird things Mrs. Greenough has packed for Daisy:

1. Energy bars that smell like vitamin pills.

2. Radishes.

3. Figs with no Newton around them.

Ms. Marshall claps her hands, and some hair falls in her face. Her special braid never lasts all day.

"Okay, boys and girls, girls and boys!" she says. She tries to be fair. "Nutrition break—but *quietly*, I beg of you."

Everyone jumps up and charges into the cloakroom to get a snack. I wiggle my way in next to Daisy, whose arm is stuck deep into her backpack. "Hi," I say, feeling shy.

LaVon is staying away from us. She is

hanging out in the corner, looking down at the floor like it is very, very interesting.

Daisy turns around to look at me.

Marcus is standing right there. "Ooh, fight, fight!" he says, sounding happy.

"Shut up," Daisy and I say to him at exactly the same time. We give little smiles to each other—but only for a second. Marcus looks disappointed and he turns to leave.

"Hi," Daisy says to me, as though Marcus never said a word. But then she lifts her chin up, like she is expecting me to say something mean.

"Hi," I say back, smiling big to show her that I am friendly.

Uh-oh—that makes three times we said hi to each other, which is one time too many. I hope that Daisy didn't notice.

"Want some of my pita bread?" I ask her.

A funny look seems to fly across Daisy's face. It is as though she wants to keep our fight going and say, *No! KEEP your old pita bread!* But at the same time she looks like she wants us to be friends again!

Or maybe she's just hungry. Anyway, she says, "Okay, sure."

Stevie Braddock interrupts us. "You don't want Lily's stupid old pita bread," he tells Daisy. "Hey," he says, like it is his duty to remind her, "she knocked you over and stomped you flat, remember?"

"I did not!" I say. "I didn't stomp her flat, anyway."

Daisy just stares at Stevie for a second, and then she starts laughing. "Mind your own beeswax, Stevie B."

That is a funny thing for her to say,

because Stevie is always saying that exact same thing to everyone in our class.

"Yeah, *Stevie*," I say like an echo. We stare at him until he creeps away. LaVon stares, too.

But then Daisy and I can't think of what to say to each other next. The cloakroom is almost empty now.

I don't see Hilary anywhere.

"Hey, want to go outside and eat?" Daisy asks me, as if it is a brand-new idea. Like we don't do that almost every day.

"Sure," I say. I am so happy that she is talking to me again!

* * *

There was rain again last night, and the playground is still dark and wet. It is a cloudy day, but there are a few streaks of sunshine zigzagging across the yard.

I look over to the place where Daisy fell

down. There is a black puddle there now. Maybe the rain has washed away all the bad things that happened that day.

It's funny, but I can barely picture what *did* happen there! It's almost as though Marcus and Stevie tell the story about our fight better than I do, even if they get it wrong. Their goofy stories are probably what people will remember about my famous fight with Daisy Greenough.

Which reminds me, I haven't told Daisy that I am sorry for ruining her surprise!

"I'm sorry for ruining your surprise," I say, handing her some triangles of pita bread. I take a hunk of string cheese from my snack bag and start to pull it apart—so I can share that with her, too. Also, the cheese tastes better that way.

"Anybody want some crackers?" LaVon asks, finally joining us. Maybe she is trying to change the subject, because now it is obvious that she has talked to me about Daisy's valentine-making party.

But Daisy doesn't seem to care if I know about the party. "That's okay," she says. "And I *do* want a cracker. Anybody want a bite of brown rice and tofu squares?" she offers, opening a little container. The wind ruffles her yellow bangs.

"Sure," I lie, while LaVon looks up at the clouds like she is studying them. Daisy hands me a blue plastic spoon. I try to swallow the rice and tofu without chewing any of it. *Glunk.*

I wait for Daisy to talk about her great idea for the valentine-making party, but she doesn't say a word. I look at LaVon, but LaVon is still gazing up at the sky.

LaVon won't look at me. That's weird.

I try to think of something to say to

Daisy and LaVon. I look across the playground, and—there is Hilary, over near the trash cans, leaning against the fence.

She is all alone.

I get a funny feeling in my tummy when I look at her. "Hey, you guys," I say, "you know who's nice? Hilary Mitchell! Maybe she can eat lunch with us later on."

LaVon smiles for a second. Her face reminds me of the sunlight that is zipping across the playground, but then she looks at Daisy. Daisy is shaking her head *no,* and she looks very serious. Her long yellow bangs swing back and forth. "Hilary is dumb," Daisy announces.

"No, she's not," I say, but my heart is thunking hard under my red sweater. "Hilary is almost as good as Marcus in arithmetic, and you know it."

"Well, but her *hair* is dumb," Daisy says, like she is explaining something that even a baby can understand.

The three of us turn to stare at Hilary's long skinny braids. From here, they don't look any thicker than a pencil.

Now, across the yard, Hilary is the one who is gazing up at the sky. I guess she sees us looking at her.

"I don't think her hair is dumb," I say.

"LaVon does," Daisy tells me.

"Urk," LaVon says. Her hand goes up to her own braids, which are shorter and puffier than Hilary's are.

Daisy sniffs. "*You* eat lunch with Hilary Mitchell if you want to so bad, Lily," she says. "Me and LaVon don't care. Do we, LaVon? We'll eat all by ourselves."

"Urk," LaVon says again. She looks at me, and her eyes are saying, *Sorry!*

But I am just wishing that I could press some invisible rewind button and erase the last few minutes. Before nutrition break, all I was worried about was making friends with Daisy again so we could have that party! And now she doesn't even want to eat lunch with me.

If I invite Hilary Mitchell, that is.

I look over at Hilary again, who is snapping the lid back on her snack container. Well, I think—she doesn't look so lonely. Maybe she's used to eating alone by now.

LaVon clears her throat. "What if Hilary—"

"Shut up, LaVon," Daisy says.

LaVon shuts up, and I start to get mad. I think I am also getting another

stomach-ache. "Stop bossing everybody around," I say to Daisy.

"I'm not bossing," Daisy says. "Am I, LaVon?"

"Urk," LaVon says for the third time. Now when she looks at me, her eyes say *Save me!*

"You shouldn't let Daisy do that to you," I tell LaVon.

"Shut up, *Lily,* " Daisy says this time. "Now who's trying to be the boss? And anyway—who cares what you say?" she tells me. "You and your stupid pita bread."

"Well, you and your stupid tofu rice!" I say back at her. Hah!

Kids are looking in our direction as though they just *know* we are having another fight.

And then the bell rings.

CHAPTER SEVEN
A Party!

"Yow, yow, *yow!*" I yell while Mommy combs the snarls out of my wet hair. We are in the bathroom, but the door is open. It is Sunday morning.

"Hold still, Lily," my mommy says. "I'm just about done."

"It hurts!" I tell her.

Casey looks up from the big chair next to the telephone, where he is reading the funnies in his T-shirt and sweatpants. "Hair doesn't have any feelings in it," he says. "If it did, nobody would ever get a haircut."

"Well, *something* hurts. *Yow!*"

"Lily's skin is very sensitive, Case," my mommy calls out to him. "Don't forget, she's a fragile little blossom."

The lid is down on the toilet and Mommy is sitting on it. Her legs clamp around me like she is a lobster while she tries to comb my hair, and she has started muttering things under her breath.

"Yow," I remind her.

Mommy's legs hold me even tighter, and she swivels me around so she can look me in the eye. "Sweetie, you're going to have to get a haircut if you keep fussing like this every time I comb your hair."

"I don't want short hair," I say. "None of the girls in my class has short hair. Do you want me to look like a *boy?*"

Mommy sighs and starts combing again. "I just want another cup of coffee, that's all," she says. "But I also want you to be as bright and clean as a brand-new penny for

Valentine's Day tomorrow. There, I'm done! Now it's time for the hair dryer."

"But that's too loud!" I say. "The noise hurts my ears."

"It's raining outside," Mommy tells me. "You're not running around all morning with wet hair, Lily Hill. And I need to trim your toenails today, too."

Trim my toenails! That is such a lie, because trimming is what you do when you decorate a Christmas tree. That means you put ornaments and tinsel on it! But my mommy is really going to *cut* my toenails.

Cut, using very sharp scissors!

Oh, sure, the scissors are round on the ends, but they could still hurt you.

"Not her toenails!" Casey yells from the living room.

For once I agree with Case. *"Not my toenails!"* I cry, like an echo.

"Casey, bring in the hair dryer, would you?" Mommy calls out to him, ignoring his toenail remark. "I'm afraid to let go of Lily."

Huh! Just because I hid under her bed that *one time*.

I can hear Casey sigh, even though I am in the bathroom and he is in the living room. "Oh, okay," he says, and he throws the funnies onto the floor. He goes into Mommy's bedroom and then appears at the bathroom door with the hair dryer.

It looks like a shiny black space gun.

"Don't shoot me with that!" I beg, holding my hands in front of my face.

"Oh, Lily, for heaven's sake," Mommy grumbles, plugging it in.

Rrrrrrrrrrrrr! goes the hair dryer.

Rrrrrrrrrrrr! A blast of hot air hits me right on the nose. I squinch my eyes shut and cover my ears, but I can hear Mommy saying something. "What?" I ask, opening one eye and one ear.

"I *said*, how would you like some pretty pink polish on your nicely trimmed toenails for Valentine's Day tomorrow? As a special treat!" she calls out over the noise of the dryer.

"Polish?" I ask, amazed. "I get to wear nail polish?" The reason that I am surprised is because I have been wanting to wear nail polish for a long time. Mommy always said no. Actually, she said, *No way*.

Now, though, she laughs. "Sure—you can wear polish on your toenails," she tells me. "It's a special occasion," Mommy adds. She turns off the dryer.

"You're bribing her!" Casey yells from the

living room. "How come you're not getting *me* a treat? Is it because I'm too good? Because I could be bad, you know."

"Don't worry—I'll share," I yell out to him. "You can wear some of *my* polish!"

I can hear the newspaper rustle in the living room, but Case doesn't say another word.

"I'll tell you what—I'll get you a new felt-tip marker for your cartooning, Case. And maybe some drawing paper," Mommy says to him. "We're going to the drugstore anyway, to buy valentines for Lily's class."

Case appears at the door again. "That's more like it," he says with a big smile.

"Now you're bribing *him*," I complain.

Mommy laughs. "I'm just waiting for someone to try to bribe *me,*" she says. "I'd welcome it with open arms!"

Open arms. That is a funny expression,

I think, except I am not laughing, because I just remembered that Daisy and LaVon are probably having fun together this weekend—without me. Maybe right this very minute! Maybe Daisy welcomed LaVon with open arms. I make a face just thinking about it.

"Did I pull your hair, sweetie?" Mommy asks.

"Nuh-uh," I say, and then I get an idea. "I was only thinking that it might be fun to *make* valentines," I say.

Mommy frowns. "I told you, Lily—we don't have the time this year," she says. "It'll take you long enough just to print everyone's names on the envelopes."

"But it's my first year at my new school!" I say. "Other kids are making cards," I add.

I don't say who.

"Lily might *have* to make her cards, Mom,"

Casey says. "There probably won't be any packages of valentines left. Or only the lame ones, like with duckies and kittens."

"I'm not giving the kids in my class any baby stuff!" I warn everyone—even though I *like* pictures of duckies and kittens. I wouldn't mind getting some.

"I could help her make the valentines if we get some construction paper at the drugstore," Case offers. "Maybe Ned could come over and help, too. He could do some of the lettering."

"It sounds like a party!" Mommy says. "Could you and Ned really help out, Case?"

Case nods.

"It's not really a party if I don't get to invite any friends," I say in my saddest voice.

"Invite Daisy and LaVon, why don't you?" Mommy suggests.

"I can't," I mumble.

Casey looks at me as if he feels sorry for me. "Ned's your friend," he says. "Sort of."

"He's *your* friend," I tell him.

"Well," Mommy says, "what about asking someone else from your class, Lily? We have everyone's phone number."

I think for a moment. "Even Hilary Mitchell's?" I ask.

"I'll go look," Casey volunteers. He disappears but then comes back with the list of phone numbers. "Mitchell, Hilary," he reports. "She lives over on American Street."

"That's close to Bainbridge," Mommy says. "In fact, it's just around the corner from us." She takes the list from Case and studies it.

"Hey, don't forget to trim my toenails," I remind her. Because *I want that polish*.

CHAPTER EIGHT
Me, Bossy?

Hilary and I follow Case and Ned up the stairs to our apartment. She *does* live close to me—in a little house that looks like it belongs to a doll family. I wish *we* still had a house.

Ned looks back over his shoulder at us and grins, then he stumbles a little on one of the stairs. His pants are too big, that's why, and also he's holding a paper bag from the drugstore. It's not that he's clumsy or anything.

The paper bag has all this cool stuff inside—like construction paper, two kinds of glue, and doilies, which Casey treated us to. And Hilary brought over some stickers she's been saving!

I have stickers, too—and some even have fuzz on them. But I'm saving those for my most special valentine cards.

"Watch out for that step," Ned warns us, and he pushes his glasses up higher on his nose with his one free hand.

Hilary is feeling shy, I can tell. She is walking right behind me—so close that I am afraid of kicking her if I run up the stairs too fast. She is wearing black leggings and a long yellow sweatshirt with black stripes and a pouch pocket in the front. There are yellow yarn bows around her skinny braids.

I am wearing all-pink clothes because tomorrow is Valentine's Day! And guess what? Underneath my sneakers and socks, my toenails are covered with pink polish!

"Hi, guys," Mommy says as we walk

through the door. She is holding a box of brownie mix in one hand.

"Brownies!" Case says, and Ned smiles some more. He puts the drugstore bag on our kitchen table.

"Lily?" Mommy says to me, and she lifts up one eyebrow—which I cannot do no matter how hard I try.

When she does that, it means she is reminding me about something.

"Oh, yeah," I say. "Mommy, this is Hilary Mitchell from my class. Hilary, this is my mommy, Mrs. Hill."

"How do you do?" Hilary whispers, staring down at her feet. Then she bites her lower lip and holds out her hand like she is about to get a shot at the doctor's office.

Mommy shakes her hand. "I'm so glad

you could come," she says. "And you live so close! If this wasn't such a big city, we would have known we were neighbors. But Lily has told me a lot about you."

I am surprised when she says this last part, because it is a fib. I don't think I have ever even said Hilary's name out loud in this apartment before, not until a couple of hours ago.

"I'm just about to put the brownie pan in the oven," Mommy tells us. She peers at the back of the box and then sets the timer.

Casey is getting out all of our art supplies, including his collection of markers, which he dumps onto the kitchen table. "Should we tell you when the timer goes off?" Case asks Mommy.

"No—I think you can handle it," she says. "I'm going to be in the bedroom doing

some work. Save me a brownie, though—
I'll need to keep up my strength!"

"Okay," Casey and I say together, but I
am already thinking about the valentines I
am going to make.

"You sit there," I tell Hilary, and she sits
down and scoots her chair in close to the
table. She folds her hands together, like she
is waiting for a spelling test to begin.

"Some of these colors are kind of
wimpy," Case announces, carefully tearing
sheets of construction paper from the pad.
"This one's almost gray."

"They always hide the bad colors in the
middle," Ned says.

"Hilary doesn't mind," I tell them. "She
likes those colors—don't you, Hilary?"

"I guess," Hilary whispers.

Ned leans over to say something in

Case's ear. "Can she talk?" I hear him ask. Case nods. "I think so," he says quietly.

"Here, Hilary," I say, and I give her six pieces of construction paper. "We each get six. We can cut them up and make tiny cards—enough for everyone in our class." It's kind of fun being the boss for once.

Hilary looks over at my six pieces of paper. I have beautiful colors—purple, pink, red, white, black, and green. "Can we trade?" she asks, holding out a piece of yellow paper that is so pale it looks like someone left it out in the rain for a week. "I want some pink paper."

"But I don't like that color," I tell her.

"No one does," Case says. "Why don't you guys go halfsies on the pink?"

"Because I need it all," I say. *Duh.*

Case gives me a dirty look. "Take some

of *my* pink," he says to Hilary. He cuts a piece of construction paper in half.

"Here's some yellow," Hilary says, sliding a piece of neatly cut paper in his direction.

We stay pretty quiet while we do the cutting and folding part, because you have to do it exactly right. The smell of brownies fills our apartment, and my stomach starts gurgling. "Hilary's stomach is growling," I tell Case and Ned, before they tease me. "I can hear it."

"It is not!" Hilary says, blushing as pink as the construction paper she is cutting.

"I was just kidding," I say, and I smile at Ned because I don't want him to think I am being mean to my new friend Hilary. He gives me a funny look.

Hilary is making the neatest folded

cards you ever saw, but she doesn't look as if she is having very much fun.

"Who wants some doilies?" Case asks. He starts peeling them apart, and they make a tiny noise that sounds like the crunch of potato chips.

"I do!" I say. "I want doilies!"

"I do, too," Hilary whispers. Case hands her the first ones.

"You have to be careful with those," I tell her. "They're very delicate."

"Well, they are delicate, but we have tons," Case says. "Why are you being so bossy, Lily?" he adds, handing me a couple of doilies.

Me, bossy? I'm only trying to be helpful, that's all! "I'm not bossy," I say. "Daisy's the one who's bossy—isn't she, Hilary?" I smile at Hilary to show everyone how friendly and not-bossy I am.

Hilary nods her head, but she doesn't say anything.

Ding! The timer goes off. "Oh, boy!" Ned says, looking at the oven.

"I'll get the brownies out," Casey says, and he gets up and puts two oven mitts on his hands. "Watch out!" he says, squeezing his fingers together, like the mitts are hand puppets that are about to bite someone. He starts walking in my direction. "Watch out!" he says again, this time to *me*. He gives me a private look that says, *Quit being rude to a guest!*

"You'd better not pinch me," I yell.

Hilary ducks her head and smiles.

"Pinch, pinch!" Casey says, doing it again.

"I'm going to yell for Mommy," I warn him.

Ned is starting to look worried. "Don't let the brownies burn," he tells my brother.

"Okay—but *watch out*," Case says, and he gives me that look again. The scolding one.

"*You* watch out," I mutter. I pick up the glue stick. "Here's how you use this," I say to Hilary.

"I know how to use it," she tells me. Her voice isn't so whispery anymore.

"Well, but you don't want to smear on too much, or you'll waste it," I say.

"I know how to work a glue stick!" Hilary says again. She is starting to get a little cranky, if you ask me.

I grab the squeeze bottle of white glue. "This is just for glitter," I tell her.

"I wasn't even going to use any," Hilary says. "Not yet."

"Okay—but when you do use it, the secret is not to squeeze too hard," I say.

Casey bangs down the pan of brownies on top of the stove, takes off the oven mitts, and turns a dial on the front of the stove. "You *are* being bossy," he announces.

"You shut up!" I say. "I am not!"

Ned is looking as though he wishes he was someplace else. He gets like that whenever Casey and I yell.

Hilary clears her throat a little. We all turn to look at her. "You are *too* being bossy, Lily," she finally says, blushing some more.

"Well, but it's my glue!" I say. I snatch the glue stick away from her hands. "And it's my glue stick, too!"

"I know that," she says. She stacks up all her folded papers like she is about to take them home. "You're worse than Daisy," she tells me.

Worse than Daisy? "Thanks a lot!" I yell. "Why did you even come to my house if you were just going to be mean to me?"

Hilary jumps to her feet so fast that the chair almost tips over. "I thought we would have fun," she says.

She's not having fun.

I'll bet Daisy and LaVon are having fun!

"Maybe we *would* have fun," I tell her, "if–if–if you didn't come over here looking like a *wasp!*" I point my finger at her leggings and yellow and black sweatshirt. "And you can't eat any of the brownies that my mommy baked if you don't start acting nicer!" I stomp my foot.

Hilary stomps her foot, too. "Well, my

daddy says that making brownies from a box isn't even baking—it's just *stirring!*"

Case cracks up laughing, and so does Ned.

"What in the world is going on in here? I heard yelling," Mommy says, walking into the kitchen.

"It was Hilary," I tell her. "She just insulted your cooking."

"I did *not,*" Hilary whispers. Oh great— she looks like she is about to start crying.

Mommy frowns—but at *me,* not at Hilary! "Do I need to talk to you in private, Miss Hill?" she asks.

"*Yes,*" Casey says.

I wish I could tell him to shut up, but I can't. Mommy would *really* frown at me, then! And talk to me in private forever. "No," I say to Mommy. "That's okay."

Mommy narrows her eyes as though she is trying to decide something. Then she smiles at Hilary and says, "Something certainly smells good in here. How about a brownie?"

"She doesn't want one," I say. "Our brownies aren't good enough for Hilary. Her daddy is a *chef.*"

"Lily!" Mommy says, frowning again.

"He's a *chef?*" Case and Ned say together, like it is such a big deal.

By now, Hilary has grabbed all her folded papers from the kitchen table. She starts stuffing them in her sweatshirt pouch. "I'm going home!" she says in a wobbly voice.

"Oh, Hilary—*no,*" Mommy says, all upset. "Don't do that, honey! Everything will be all right—and we want you to stay."

"Let her go," I tell Mommy. "She said bad things about your brownies, so she can't have any!"

"Be quiet, Lily—this very *second,*" Mommy says.

I zip my mouth shut and fold my arms tight across my chest.

"I didn't say bad things," Hilary tells Mommy. "I only said that making brownies from a box wasn't really baking, that's all." It looks like she is about to faint, practically.

Hah—it serves her right!

"Come on, stay," Casey says, starting to cut the brownies. "We want you to stay. Right, Ned?"

I shut my mouth even tighter. I bite down on my lips to keep them from talking.

Ned nods his head. "You can even stomp your foot again," he says to Hilary.

"You don't have to eat any brownies if you don't want to," Case tells her.

"I think we have some graham crackers," Mommy says, going over to the cupboard. "They're not homemade, though."

"I never said I didn't want a box brownie," Hilary says, watching Case lift the dark brown crumbly squares onto a plate.

I can't stand this! I jump to my feet. "Well, she's not getting any," I inform everyone. "Hilary is not my friend anymore," I say. My heart is beating very fast.

"Oh, Lily, don't be ridiculous," Mommy says. "Just because someone stands up to you doesn't mean she can't be a friend."

"Yeah—in fact, I think Hilary should get an award," Case says, plunking the brownie plate down on the table. "I think I'll make one for her right now!" he adds.

"And I'll pour some lemonade for you guys," Mommy says. "I made it from a can, Hilary—but would you like a glass?"

Hilary slides back onto her chair and nods her head. "I hate real lemonade," she says. "It's always too sour." She takes her folded valentine papers out of her pouch. They are only a little bit bent.

My heart is slowing down, but I keep on standing.

"Is your father really a chef?" Ned asks Hilary.

Hilary looks at me, and then she nods her head again. Mommy hands her a glass of our pink lemonade. "I'm sorry I was so rude, Mrs. Hill," Hilary says. "I just got mad, that's all."

"Oh, honey—think nothing of it," my mommy says, touching her shoulder. "I don't blame you a bit for losing your temper. And your father's quite right, you know. Real baking is an art."

I sit down and carefully cut a doily in half. I think I will put a pig sticker right in the middle of it and make it look like a little pig angel.

"But I like brownies-from-a-box," Hilary says in a hurry. "We just never get to have them at my house, that's all."

"Well, you can have them here," Mommy says, laughing again. "Can't she, Lily?"

Everyone turns to look at me.

"I guess," I say. I sneak a look at Hilary, and then I push the glue stick toward her. "Here," I say. "This is for the doilies. If you want."

"Thank you," Hilary tells me, and she puts the glue stick next to her valentines. Then she reaches for a brownie.

CHAPTER NINE
I'm Sorry

Pretty soon the brownies and lemonade are all gone. Case and Ned get bored and start goofing around, throwing doilies at each other and stuff. They finally decide to go outside, and so Hilary and I are left alone in the kitchen. Mommy is back in her room.

"Your brother is funny," Hilary says as soon as the front door closes.

I put a heart sticker on a valentine and pound it flat with my fist. *Bam!* "He's okay," I agree.

"Is Ned his best friend?" Hilary asks.

I peek at her, because I have just been thinking about best friends—and how I don't have any, anymore. And I know now that there is no way I can boss Hilary into being my new best friend. "I guess he is," I say. "I mean, Case doesn't *call* him that, or anything. But they hang out together a lot."

Hilary sighs and brushes some loose pink glitter into a little pile on the tabletop.

"What's the matter?" I say to her.

She shrugs her shoulders, then she looks at me all of a sudden. "Are you in trouble with your mom because of me?" she asks.

"A little bit," I admit, pounding down another sticker. "She'll probably give me a talking-to after you leave. But it's no big deal. It just lasts a long time, that's all."

"I'm sorry," Hilary says, shrinking down in her chair a little.

"That's okay," I tell her. "It happens to me all the time. And—and I guess I *was* being kind of bossy," I add in a rush. "I'm sorry," I say. I hold up a finished valentine and stare at it, hard.

"That's okay," Hilary says. "You didn't mean to be bossy."

I think about that. "Yes, I did," I finally tell her. "I wanted to see what being the boss felt like," I say.

Hilary looks curious. "What *did* it feel like?" she asks.

Now *I'm* the one who shrugs. "I don't know. Kind of good, in a way," I admit, "because usually I'm the one who gets bossed around."

"I know. Me too," Hilary says.

I fold a couple of valentines. "Am I really bossier than Daisy?" I ask Hilary.

She laughs. "No one is bossier than Daisy," she says to me.

"Yeah, but at least kids do what she says," I tell her, thinking about LaVon.

"Nobody does what I say," I add.

"Maybe you should get a dog," Hilary suggests.

"I *wish*," I say.

"We've got a dog. A little one," Hilary tells me.

"You *do?* How little?" I ask her, suddenly imagining a dog so tiny—like an eraser! —that you could put him in your pocket and take him to school. And no one would know. Now, *that* would be cool.

Hilary holds her hands about as far apart as a banana is long. "So big," she says. "He's a miniature dachshund. His name is Rocky. My dad named him," she says, like she is apologizing.

But I think Rocky is a good name for a dog.

"Want to come over to my house and

see him?" Hilary asks. "We could dress him up in doll clothes," she adds.

Like she has to *convince* me to come!

"Sure!" I say. "When?"

"Well, what about now?" Hilary says, flipping her braids back.

I jump up so fast that some stickers fall off the table. "I'll go ask my mom!" I tell her.

"But won't she say no?" Hilary asks, looking worried. "If you're in trouble?"

"I'm not in *that* much trouble," I say. "Mommy wants me to have friends! And she can give me my talking-to after I get home," I add, excited. "There'll be plenty of time tonight."

Hilary grins at me. "You're funny," she says.

"But not bossy, right?" I ask.

"Not anymore," she tells me.

CHAPTER TEN
Valentine's Day

It is Valentine's Day—at last.

We each hold a shoebox covered with gift-wrap paper. Ms. Marshall helped us decorate them last Friday. My box is dark blue with turquoise flowers on it.

At our school, the rule is that if you bring valentines to class, you must give one to everybody. Even the kids who say they hate Valentine's Day bring valentines for good luck—because they want to *get* valentines. They want to get *lots* of valentines!

We all have the cards we brought from home stacked on our desks.

"Girls and boys, boys and girls, put your shoeboxes against the far wall," Ms. Marshall says, trying to brush back her falling-down braid. "You may deliver your valentines during Sustained Silent Reading. I'll call your names in groups of six."

We all walk over to the wall, carrying our boxes and smiling big at each other. Even Ollie Howard does, and he hates the whole class, I sometimes think. But this is a day when you are nice to everyone, just in case.

"Your shoebox looks pretty," the girl next to me says shyly. Her name is Lupe.

"Thanks," I say to her. "Yours does, too." I am telling the truth, because even though Hilary is the neatest person in our class, Lupe is the best artist—after LaVon. And I hate to admit it, but Ollie Howard is number three. Marcus *could* be number four, but he goes racing through every art project like there is a bear chasing him.

I am somewhere in the middle with a whole bunch of other kids. But that's okay. You have lots of company when you are in the middle.

We line up the boxes very neatly and return quietly to our seats. I give Hilary a secret smile, but my heart is pounding *thunk, thunk* because this is such a special afternoon. My heart pounds right on top of my stomach, which is still full from lunch. It is *very* full from lunch, in fact! I ate an extra sandwich—because Mrs. Greenough is bringing a Valentine's Day snack for us later on.

Alfalfa sprouts is my guess.

Ms. Marshall starts calling out names, and I pretend to read. I am really thinking about Valentine's Day, though. I think it is the most important holiday in school, even though grownups have forgotten that. It is an important day because it counts how many friends you have and how much they like you.

That's why all us kids are so nervous today—because even though there is a rule about giving everyone a valentine, and even though you can't exactly say, *Hi, I hate you!* on any of the cards, there are lots of secret messages that you can send. Like if you buy someone a fancy drugstore card or make a great big card with fuzzy or puffy stickers on it, that is saying, *I like you a lot!*

If you pass out those tiny cartoony cards, well—it depends what you write on them. If you write nothing or if you just make question marks or something on the backs of them, those cards mean *You're okay, I guess.*

But if you write something on the backs of the cards, that's better. That means *You're okay!* without the *I guess.*

That's good.

And if you make your own valentines, or some of them at least, I think that's very good! Even though Daisy thought of doing it first.

But Hilary and I made some really cool valentines, and I think the kids in our class will love them! We used every-thing—glitter, doilies, our extra-nice stickers, and some little googly plastic eyes that Ned surprised us with. Our cards say, *Look at this!* and *I like you* and <u>*I'm*</u> *okay,* all at the same time. Anyone would love to get a valentine like that.

"Earth to Lily, Earth to Lily," someone is saying. It is Ms. Marshall.

"Here!" I cry out, and everyone laughs, even the teacher.

"I'm not taking roll, Miss Hill," she says, shaking her head. More hair falls down out of her braid. "I was just calling your name so that you could deliver your valentines."

"Oh, okay," I tell her, and I grab my big stack of cards and hop out of my chair.

At the back of the room, five other kids are already prowling up and down the line of shoeboxes, stuffing cards into them. Hilary is one of them. She gives me a great big smile.

Hi, my mouth says back at her without making any sound.

Marisa, Timothy, George. I deliver the valentines. *Ollie.* I made a card for Ollie, but I didn't sign it.

Hilary! I waited until last night to make

her card. I used three of my best fuzzy panda stickers on it and signed it *Your new friend Lily.* Casey told me the spelling.

LaVon. I made a special card for her, with a teddy bear sticker right on the front—to match her backpack! And I put silver glitter around the edges, because LaVon likes glitter. I signed it *LILY* in big letters, and I drew a giant heart around the letters so she would know for sure who it was from—and that I still like her.

And *Daisy.* I put three glittery heart stickers on her card, because she and LaVon and I used to be three best friends. And even though Daisy is bossy, and even though we had a fight, and even though she is being dumb about Hilary, that doesn't mean I can't still like her. Does it?

There—finished! I have delivered my last valentine. The other five kids in my group have sat down already, and I know I should sit down, too. But first . . .

I peek over at Ms. Marshall. She is busy helping Ollie Howard sound out words in his reader. And so—

My shoebox is sitting crooked on the floor. I tiptoe over to straighten it. And while I'm there, I take a little peek inside.

Yes-s-s! I have tons of valentines already! Well, not tons, exactly, but at least I can say for sure that not everybody in my class hates me. And lots of my valentines have writing on them, and there are even some homemade ones with stickers and drawings and everything!

My finger reaches out to push some tiny cards away so I can see the drawing on one of the bigger cards. And then all of a sudden I feel frozen, just like a Popsicle.

The drawing shows two stick-figure girls. You can tell they are supposed to be friends, because they are holding hands.

One of the girls has long skinny braids hanging down to her knees, almost. She has a silly expression on her face. Both girls do, really. And the other girl has messy brown hair all over her head, tons of it. And there are dots all over her face. Those are supposed to be freckles.

Because that girl is supposed to be me.

Somehow, I make my finger lift open the card. Inside, it just says, *Too bad!*

And there is a drawing of a daisy underneath.

CHAPTER ELEVEN
P.S.

There is still time for me to accidentally smash Daisy's shoebox flat with my red sneaker. I'm mad enough to do it!

But I don't.

There is still time for me to take my nice valentine out of Daisy's box, but I don't do that, either. And it's not just because I'm scared about getting caught—although Ms. Marshall does seem to pop up whenever I even think about doing something bad.

But all of the good things I was just thinking about Daisy are still true. We *were* best friends for a while, her and me and LaVon. We *did* have fun together. And I *do* like them both, even though Daisy is acting mean now and LaVon is too chicken to tell her to quit it—and that makes me sad.

The weird thing is, even though I can sort of remember *how* my fight with Daisy happened, I still don't know *why* it happened. Maybe it's like I said before—I'm just the leftover from three kids trying to be best friends. Maybe...

"Lily?" Ms. Marshall says. Uh-oh, she has crept up behind me again. "Would you care to rejoin the class?"

"Okay," I tell her.

✳ ✳ ✳

P.S. I am in bed now, counting my valentines. I got twenty-eight valentines out of thirty-two kids, plus one of a kitten from Ms. Marshall, which makes twenty-nine. Two kids were absent, so that means only two people didn't give me a valentine. Phooey on them!

And I got six homemade valentines, which is a lot.

1. There's Daisy's card—well, you already know about that one.

Oh—her mother surprised everyone and brought in real cupcakes for our Valentine's Day treat, with real frosting on them! So you can't always tell—about grownups anyway, and maybe about kids, too.

2. Another homemade card is from Ollie Howard, I'm sure of it. There is a skunk sticker on the front, and inside it says, *P.U. U Stink!* The skunk is kind of cute, though.

3. And there's a funny valentine from Marcus. It has a glitter frog sticker on it,

and Marcus knows I love frogs. He even drew a picture of a lily pad around the sticker and signed his name. Marcus is okay.

4. And Hilary made me a card in secret, just like I did for her! It is very beautiful, and she used a whole doily on it, and she drew a picture of Rocky on the front. Wearing a baby bonnet. Inside are the words *Love, Hilary* written in extra-curly letters with flowers all around them.

5. Lupe made me a pretty card with tissue paper hearts glued on the front. I like Lupe. Hey, maybe she can be friends with me and Hilary someday!

6. LaVon's valentine is the best, though. You can tell she spent a long time on it. It is made out of pink construction paper, and the edges of the card look like they

were dipped in solid gold glitter. She must have used half a jar just for me! And LaVon traced three hearts on the front of the card with a purple marker and drew lacy loops around the outside of each heart.

Here's what she wrote inside the card :

I guess that someone had to help her with the spelling, too, and one of the hearts is kind of jiggly, but it's still my favorite valentine.

I don't know why, exactly.